W9-AJT-264

GOING WEST

Ma

STORY BY
**Martin
WADDELL**

Kate

Pa

PICTURES BY
**Philippe
DUPASQUIER**

Louisa

Peter

Harper & Row, Publishers

EAU CLAIRE DISTRICT LIBRARY

88206

Going West
Copyright © 1983 by Martin Waddell and Philippe Dupasquier
First published in Great Britain by Andersen Press Ltd., London W.1.
All rights reserved. Printed in England by W. S. Cowell Ltd.

Trade ISBN 0-06-026332-6
Harpercrest ISBN 0-06-026333-4
Library of Congress Catalogue Card Number 83-48650

First American Edition

Pa gave me this Wagon Book to write our adventures.
This is our family.
Me and Ma and Pa and Louisa and Rufus and Peter.
We are going West to look for better land.

We went into town to join the others.
We are going with Mr. Crowe's wagon train.

There are lots of wagons.
Peter is on his horse. Ma is driving our wagon with Louisa.
I am walking with Pa. Pa says it is a long way to walk.

Big Chokey once had a fight with a grizzly bear. He lost his leg.
Now Big Chokey has a wooden leg he keeps things in.
Here he is, showing me the things in his leg.
This is our camp.

Louisa and Mrs. Sullivan drank bad water.
They got sick. I didn't get sick.
Pa and Mr. Sullivan are asking Mr. Crowe,
the Wagon Master, what to do.

The others went on.
Mr. Ridger and Big Chokey and the Sullivans stayed with us.
Big Chokey will show us the way.
We will try to catch up to the others later.

Louisa is still very sick.
But Big Chokey says we must try to catch up to the others.
We are very far behind.
Now it's two weeks later, and Big Chokey has lost their trail.
There was a bad storm. We saw Indians.

EAU CLAIRE DISTRICT LIBRARY

We crossed the river. There was a lot of water.
Peter was washed away but he didn't drown. Mr. Sullivan got him.
Mr. Ridger says we must all pray for little Louisa.
I am smaller than Louisa.

Friendly Indians came to our camp.
They told us that bad Indians are trailing Mr. Crowe's wagons.
We must go another way.

Peter and Mr. Sullivan saw burning wagons. There were dead people.
Mr. Sullivan says they were in Mr. Crowe's wagon train.
It is a good thing Big Chokey's Indians told us to take another way,
or we would be dead, too.

It is very cold. We saw a dead Indian.
Big Chokey says we stole the Indians' land. They don't like us.
That is why they killed Mr. Crowe's people.
Mr. Sullivan went hunting. He saw live Indians.
Louisa is still very sick.

There was a blizzard. The snow stopped us.

Louisa got so sick she died.

We had to bury Louisa and leave her behind.
Mr. Ridger says God will look after Louisa
because she was so small.
Louisa was bigger than me.

Mr. Sullivan went hunting again. He didn't come back.
Ma is sick and Mrs. Sullivan is looking after her in our wagon.
Peter is driving the Sullivans' wagon.

Today we got through the pass.
We could see for miles and miles.
Big Chokey made me a fur coat to keep me warm.

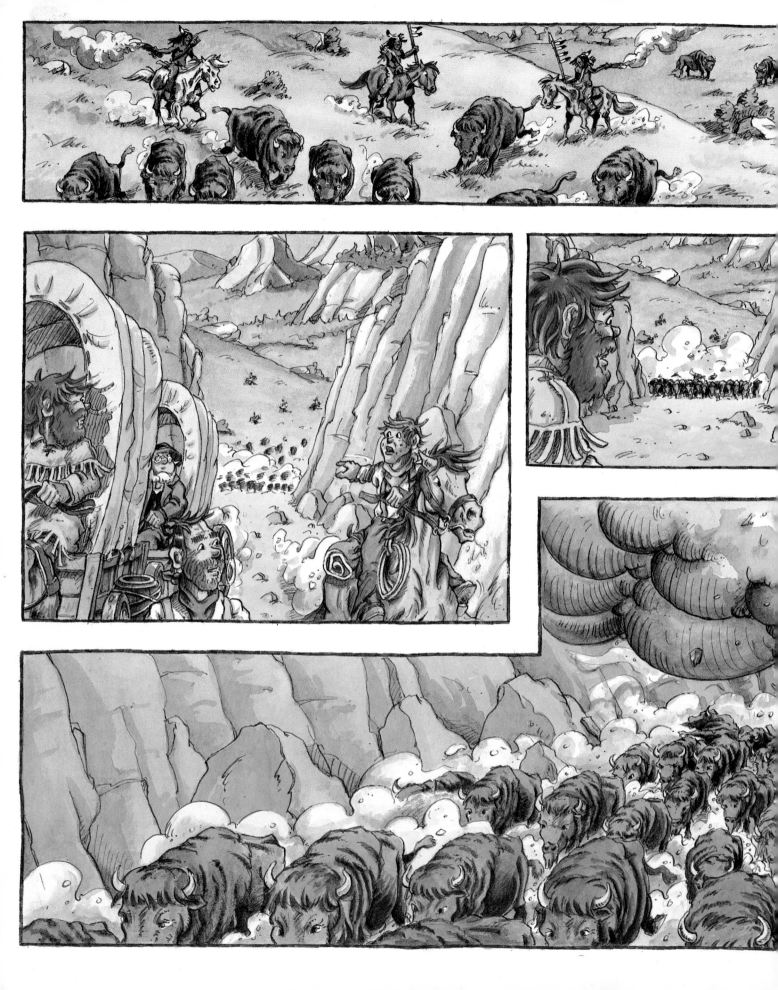

There was a buffalo stampede. We almost got killed.
Big Chokey set fire to his wagon and headed them off,
so we could get out of the way.

Some Indians attacked us. There was a bad fight.
Mr. Ridger got killed.
Ma told me to take his Bible. It is mine now.

We found a good place to build a house. It is near the town.
Mrs. Sullivan will stay with us but Big Chokey is going on.
He gave me his leg. He made himself a new one.

We are building our house.
Pa says we will be happy here.

EAU CLAIRE DISTRICT LIBRARY

DATE DUE

MY 8'86	AG 18'87	MAR 6 '97	
MY 21'86	SE 10	DEC 03 '97	
JY 22'86	MR 17'90		
JY 25'86	AP 23'90	JAN 17 '98	
AG 14'86	JY 11'90	AP 01 '00	
SE 30'86	AG 14'92	JE 29 04	
OC 8'86	MAR 21 '94	JY 08 04	
	APR 21 '94	JY 22 04	
NO 28'86	MAR 12 '96	JY 29 04	
FE 2'87	PR 15	JY 07 '05	
MY 20'87	JL 03	JY 17 06	
JY 29'87	SEP 30 98	JE 12 12	

I
Wad   Waddell, Martin
          Going west

EAU CLAIRE DISTRICT LIBRARY